A
Comedy of Conscience

" ' Leave my house ! ' "

A
Comedy of Conscience

By

S. Weir Mitchell, M.D.
LL.D. Harvard and Edinburgh

New York
The Century Co.
1903

THE DE VINNE PRESS.

List of Illustrations

[v]

A
Comedy of Conscience

A
Comedy of Conscience

I

THE friends of Serena Vernon
said that she was a spinster
by choice; she herself declared
that nature had elected her to be
a maid; but Cousin John Winterbourne said: "It is a profession
with Serena."

She spoke of herself as settled
for life, and as being thirty years
of age. Her face and figure were
as frank in representing her as

any age a man in love might
choose to set. Prophetic wisdom must have given her the
name Serena, and considerate fate
had so far done nothing to contradict the calmness of a life free from
stormy fortunes.

Serena lived tranquilly in her
own house at Denham, and con-
trived to show a fair front to the
world on an income so modest that
it would have puzzled even those
who knew her best to comprehend
how she was able to give those
delightful little dinners, which, to
tell the truth, were somewhat rare,
but entirely perfect of their kind.
She was neat in her ways, but not
too accurate; and in her dress, as

[4]

in her housekeeping, was somewhat of a mystery to her acquaintance. But, as her friend Mrs.
Clare once remarked, a large sup-
ply of old lace and unfailing good
taste will really accomplish won-
ders. She had both the lace and
the taste, and declared that she
disliked competitive exhibitions in
dress.

As a man I dare not go further
in an effort to explain what was
only a part of the mysterious at-
tractiveness of a life and ways
which were always efficient and
never in excess. She once said to
a friend that if a woman of thirty
were worth looking at, to be
dressed as if she were forty was

[5]

good policy. In fact she never did consider questions of policy, but was apt at times to make delicately humorous statements such as that I have quoted.

Miss Vernon was a quietly active member of what she spoke of as the Church, meaning the Episcopal Church, and had an unconfessed weakness for bishops, and for the clergy in general, especially if they were of the High-Church party.

A small greenhouse and a half-acre of ground took up a good deal of her time, and many a man going down the green lane in June paused to watch the tall woman in gray, in her wide hat, with basket and scissors, busy among the fast-

coming roses. Although a reader
with wide sympathies and eager
curiosity, she read only such books
as she could afford to buy, or such
as were sent her by John Winterbourne; for, being generally reticent, she was shy of explaining
that she disliked to handle the
books of public libraries because of
being distressingly imaginative as
to where and in what hands they
had been.

She was, as you may have
guessed, a gentlewoman, and possessed manners which, like her
dress, were neat and free from any
over-anxious desire to please. She
kept a cook and an antique maid,
but she felt that she was not yet

old enough to allow herself the society of a cat. Her only living relative, Cousin John Winterbourne, managed her small property, and at times gave her advice, which she often asked and rarely took. When ill, which was not often, she went to bed, sent for her other male friend, Dr. Saffron, and treated his prescriptions as she did her cousin's advice. She was intelligent, but not intellectual.

Her nearest female friend was Mrs. Clare, who had come through the storms of an ill-matched marriage into the port of a determined and well-endowed widowhood with two boys. Miss Vernon was extremely fond of children, and a

critical male acquaintance once remarked that "but for the widow's
boys Serena would have married
a clergyman. These boys were a
buffer between Serena and marriage." Miss Vernon said the re-
mark was not true and certainly
was not nice.

I should add that unobservant
people who talked for the first
time with Miss Vernon thought
her reserved and not very inter-
esting. Indeed, most of the many
men who admired the grace of her
rather tall and quite perfect figure
were apt to qualify their praise
with the statement that she was
cold.

She possessed one talent, which

[9]

she kept for herself and three or four friends. She sang admirably, and the mechanic who paused at evening to listen went on his way homeward touched as by a charm of sweetness. She underrated her skill, and never sang elsewhere than in her own house.

This quiet, pleasant life was kept in order by a delicately adjusted conscience. It ran along smoothly until the singular event took place which I have now to relate.

II

SERENA had long felt that her little drawing-room required new curtains. Twice she had saved the money needed, and twice had given it away to assist a mission to the Montana Indians, this being her favorite form of charity. Now, however, a small lot of unimproved ground had been sold, and she felt free to indulge her long-postponed desire. Accordingly, she went to the great city a few miles away, and, being hard to please, filled her little hand-bag with patterns to be considered at home, dropped into it her purse, which contained the money she had meant to use for the curtains, and took a trolley-car to return.

Miss Vernon was mildly interested as to the lives and ways of people not of her own social type, and in the brightly lighted car were many such, as it was now after dusk, and all who worked were returning to their homes.

A man who sat opposite caught her eye. He was large, coarsely featured, and had a rough, red wart on his cheek. He wore a huge shirt-pin and a glittering ring, which were, as she concluded, paste.

[12]

" A man who sat opposite caught her eye."

People got in and went out. She opened her purse to pay for her ticket of transfer, replaced it in her bag, and lifted a child to her lap. Presently the man gave his seat to a thin woman encumbered with a basket. Miss Vernon said to herself that her judgment of the man needed modification, and made mental note of her too hasty conclusion as uncharitable. As others on her side of the car left it, she moved a little, and said courteously, "There is room here." He replied, "Thank you, ma'am," and sat down.

When she reached home she went into her small library, brought out of a closet a large sheet of

white wrapping-paper, and, emptying her patterns upon it, began to
consider them. Presently, sur-
prised to miss her purse, she
searched her pocket, and, failing to
find it, knew at once that the over-
dressed fellow-passenger at her
elbow was the richer by thirty-
seven dollars and fifty cents, a
luck-penny of 1798, and a receipt
for caramel custard. Much annoyed, she shook her bag, and was
amazed to see drop out a huge
gold ring in which was set a shin-
ing stone. She was not what her
friend Mrs. Clare described as an
exclamatory person, but now she
said: "Gracious goodness! How
absurd! The paste ring that man

[16]

wore! Cousin John will say — yes, he will say, 'That comes, Rena, of your confounded way of being aggressively civil.' He did say that once, and now he will call this a mutual theft. I can always tell what John will say. It must have slipped off the man's finger."

All this was said aloud in a low tone. Then Miss Vernon rose and rang the bell.

"Fetch me hot water and soap and a finger-bowl."

When thus provided, she washed the ring with scrupulous care, and, having dried it, put it on her finger. It must have been worn as a thumb-ring, she thought. She had heard that rings were thus worn in Ger-

[17]

many. It was fit for the finger of a giant.

Finally, having set down the date in her diary with a memorandum of the facts, the comic aspect of this exchange of property overcame her. She had paid rather dear for a paste stone in a sham-gold setting. She laughed heartily, wishing she could have seen the face of the pickpocket when he discovered his loss. After this she locked up the ring in her desk and rang for tea.

III

IN the evening, after dinner, Miss
Vernon settled promptly on the
pattern she liked best, and with
dismay remembered that the money
needful to buy her curtains was lost.
How shabby the old ones looked!
She went back to her volume of
Pusey's sermons, and resolutely
dismissed the matter from her
thoughts.

When abed and about to glide
tranquilly into slumber, there arose
in her mind a sudden and amazing

reflection. What if the stone were not paste? What if it were a diamond? This absurd notion was fatal to sleep; not until the dawn appeared did she forget it in slumber. At breakfast it troubled her until she concluded to settle the matter. With this in view, she returned to the city, and walked to the shop of a jeweler where she was well known. Mr. Weldon, one of the partners, showed her into a little room and gave her a seat at a small table on which lay a large square of black velvet.

Miss Vernon said, " I have here a stone lately come into my possession. Kindly tell me if it has any value."

[20]

"Any value!" he exclaimed. "Any value, Miss Vernon? It is a diamond."

"A diamond? Are you sure?"

"Certainly."

"Then it must have some value. Is it a good stone?" Miss Vernon had a not uneducated fondness for precious stones.

"It is a white diamond of perhaps two and a half carats, worth about eight hundred dollars. If it were blood-orange it would be worth six or seven thousand. Diamonds differ. Just now the taste is for color. I would suggest resetting."

"No; kindly put it in a box."

He screwed the glass on to his

eye. "Pardon me a moment, Miss Vernon. It was set about 1838 — ye-es, 1838. This setting is French," he added. "What we call in England the hall-mark is plain." Then he called a sales-man, who thought it worth quite eight hundred and fifty dollars. "Not a lady's ring," he added, with a grin.

Miss Vernon did not wish it set, nor was she inclined to sell it. Her sole desire was to be alone to think over the situation, which her imag-ination immediately set before her conscience in a variety of bewilder-ing forms.

The jeweler put the ring in a box, and, holding it fast in her hand, Miss Vernon made haste to return home, setting aside for the time the questions that inexorable ring continued to ask whenever she allowed herself to think of it.

When alone in her library, she sat down, put the ring on the table before her, and began ingeniously to torment herself. At last she became so hopelessly perplexed that she said: " I must clear my head. I will write it down"; and this was what she wrote in her diary:

This stone is worth $800!

To whom does it belong?

Was it that man's?

Did he steal it? That is not my business. Yes, it is.

[23]

The ring is not mine.

I have it. I did not steal it.

It was not given to me. The man robbed himself. He will never come for it.

What shall I do with it? Oh, dear! what will John say? I cannot sell it, because it is not mine. I cannot return it to that rascal, because it may not be his. I hate to ask advice. Now I must. I will ask my rector, and Helen Clare, and Cousin John.

IV

SERENA knew at what hour in the afternoon she would find the Rev. Angelo King in his sacristy. She was fairly inclined toward High-Church ways, but on the subject of confession had declined to follow her clerical adviser. Once she had hurt his feelings by saying: "I will confess once for all, Mr. King, that I do not like confession."

The Rev. Angelo, who liked to

be called Father King, was not of ascetic build, and, although he fasted honestly, found himself more and more of cherubic figure as life went on. Now, as she entered, he was fully prepared by Serena's grave looks for a confession. He was disappointed when she displayed the diamond and related her scruples and difficulties, but he felt that this was at least an advance toward that emptying of a contrite soul to which he so earnestly desired to bring this fair sinner.

The sinner, observing his serious face and medieval attitude, said, smiling: "This is not an ecclesiastical confession. I have done no

[26]

"'Have you never entertained the idea of keeping the ring?'"

wrong; I want to avoid doing wrong."

He replied gravely: "Have you never entertained the idea of keeping the ring, which is not your own, and is not that sin?"

Miss Serena thought this uncalled for, and was not to be so easily trapped. "Yes, but one has to entertain many thoughts about a matter so hard to dispose of. One may entertain a thought, Mr. King, and not give it much to live on."

The rector did not like this trifling with serious matters. Miss Serena was inwardly pleased with her jest, and was sorry the audience was manifestly unappreciative.

[29]

Mr. King was silent a moment, and then said: "Why not give the money to the church? We need only seven hundred for our new reredos, for the rest we already have."

"But pardon me," said Serena. "You first remind me that the diamond is not mine, then you venture to suggest that I sin in considering it mine, and at last you advise me to give away what is not mine."

"True, quite true; but the church—" Then he paused. Clergymen get the habit of not being interrupted and of seeing only one side of a question. He added foolishly: "You have told me your doubts and confessed thoughts which you feel to be wrong."

[30]

"Bless me! Mr. King, I did not confess in your sense. I do not want absolution until I feel the need of it. I cannot give what is not mine."

"Pardon me," he replied. "I may have been hasty, but you must do something with this ring. The man will never seek to recover it. The church might agree to repay the value of it if ever it is asked for. This should put you at ease."

"But, Mr. King, suppose that I do this and the man were to come and say, 'I am here to ask for my ring.' The church would say, 'It is sold.' He might say it was a valued heirloom, and where should I be, and you? I should have led you into the sin I desire to avoid for myself."

Upon this Miss Vernon rose. The Rev. Angelo also stood, but felt, as he looked up at Miss Vernon's five feet eight of graceful figure, that a foot added to his own height might have victoriously emphasized his spiritual counsel.

Miss Vernon said, "I thank you, but I cannot take your advice. Good-by," and went out disappointed mentally and morally in her rector.

V

THE next day found Miss Vernon
in her cousin John's sitting-
room, waiting for his return from
luncheon at his club. Miss Serena
put up her glass, and, moving
about, surveyed the room with the
curiosity with which an unmarried
woman always inspects a bachelor's
belongings. There were guns and
salmon-rods in apparently useless
number. A row of fly-books re-
warded her with charming colors.
Numberless journals were there —

[33]

enviably printed British quarter-
lies, the French reviews, all manner
of illustrated papers, with books on
science, art, sport, and a few French
novels. Cousin John shot ducks in
winter, or snipe and partridges, and
wound up with tarpon-fishing; had
a brief season of idleness, then
killed salmon in June, and went to
Scotland for the grouse in August.
He read, as she knew, omnivo-
rously.

She observed with unexplained
regret that the room was beauti-
fully clean.

At last Miss Serena, having
ended her inspection, settled herself in one of a half-dozen tempt-
ing easy-chairs, picked up the

[34]

nearest book (a French novel), and fell upon a rather astonishing scene. A moment later the door opened and Cousin John appeared. He was a perfectly dressed man of thirty-eight, well built, and sturdy from out-of-door life.

"Good heavens! Rena," he laughed, glancing at the book, "you won't have a moral left."

Serena blushed. "I was about to lay it down, John."

"You will not if you read it long. The devil is apt to be amusing, especially the French devil. What can I do for you? I go to Currituck to-morrow, but if—"

"Oh, it is only a little advice

that I want. Now kindly listen to me."

Then she told the story of the ring, and, ending, put it on the table. He picked it up laughing. "I have heard nothing so good for years. The ravens were around this time, Rena. What a windfall!"

"Windfall! I do not understand you."

"Certainly. You never will allow me to help you; but just now —" he hesitated — "let me add a few hundred. I should waste it at Aix or Monte Carlo. Then you will have sixteen hundred and can have that summer in English cathedrals. I congratulate you."

[36]

"I cannot take your money, John, and I am simply amazed that you could believe that I, of all people, would spend this man's money on self-indulgence."

"Now, Rena, what stuff! He stole that from some one, the scamp."

"I suppose so; it is not mine."

"Great Scott! To whom does it, will it, shall it belong?"

"Not to me. I can't give away what is not mine."

"Whose is it, Rena?"

"The man's, I suppose, or some one's from whom he stole it."

"Then advertise: 'On return of a porte-monnaie with thirty-seven dollars and fifty cents, a penny of

Washington, date 1798, and a receipt for pickled doughnuts — ' "

" Caramel custard, John."

" Well, no matter — 'the owner will return to the person bringing it back a diamond ring, value eight hundred dollars; no questions asked. No clergymen need apply.'"

" You are rather exasperating, John. But what am I to do?"

" Why not keep the ring until something turns up?"

" How can I keep it? Nothing will turn up — nothing. It is a dreadful responsibility, and I never had one before since — " and Serena colored.

" Yes, I know, dear Rena, since long ago you said, ' John — ' "

"Please not."

"Well, I believe I promised, and we have been fast friends ever since."

"Thank you," she said gently, "but do help me a little."

"Well, pitch it into the river."

"That would be waste, and you do not mean it."

"Rena, it is you who are exasperating. Spend it on Indian missions."

"I thought of that, but it is not mine. Can't you see my trouble?"

"You have too much imagination."

"No matter what I do, John, I shall end by robbing some one."

"He will never know, Rena."

"John!"

"Well, spend it, and leave the rascal with a wart a legacy in your will — eight hundred; that ought to settle it."

"Nothing settles it. If you had even an improper fraction of a conscience, John, you would feel as I do."

"A fraction of an improper conscience. I like that. Damn it, Rena, you are incredible."

"John! I am sorry I bothered you. Good-by."

"But, Rena!"

"No, I must go," and she went out. As he conducted her to the elevator, she turned smilingly, and said: "John, I have been wanting to say that for two days."

[40]

"What?"

"The exclamation you used just now."

"Gracious, Rena, what a dear you are! Good-by. I will send you a lot of ducks."

As she walked to the station, more than ever perplexed, she said: "Well, if nothing else turns up I can advertise; not just John's absurd way. The ring is the man's, not mine. Oh, if I could only see him! Now there is nothing left except Helen Clare. A woman will see this miserable business from my side."

VI

IN the late afternoon of an October day she walked a mile to her friend's house. The widow made her welcome; the children were dismissed, and, as they sat down, her friend said:

"Serena, what is wrong? You look worried."

"Oh, I am so perplexed, dear. I really cannot see my way clear."

"And his name, dear Rena?"

"I wish I knew!"

"What on earth do you mean?"

"Mean! It is n't a man. Yes, it is a man."

Miss Serena was nearer a fit of hysterics than she had ever been in all her placid life. Her friend took her hand and said very quietly, "Tell me, my love."

Then Serena lifted her dark-gray eyes and told how she had lost her purse and got a diamond worth eight hundred dollars.

Mrs. Clare exclaimed: "How delicious! Have you it with you?"

"Yes; I am afraid to leave it at home. Here it is."

Mrs. Clare inspected this queer find. "What a monster, dear! You will have to have it reset before you can wear it."

"Wear it, Helen! Wear that creature's stone — his diamond! Think, dear, of the horror of it!"

"Upon my word, Rena, if all the big diamonds could talk there would be some tales to hear. A diamond cannot perish, and what queer scenes they must have beheld — what women, what men! How many times that diamond may have caused murder!"

"What horrible imaginations, Helen!"

"Or turned the scale against a woman's honor."

"My dear Helen!"

"And yet it is pure and beautiful and innocent; one might write the biography of a diamond."

[44]

Serena said: "You might, dear, but if you were as frank on paper as in speech your story would never get into any of the magazines."

"It is your own fault, Rena. It is you who set me going. Did ever any one tell you, Rena, that you have more imagination than is good for you?"

"No, not precisely that; but really, dear, to be serious, this diamond troubles me. It is not mine. What is to be done with it?"

"I will tell you," cried Mrs. Clare, joyously.

"I knew you would."

"Such a piece of good fortune! Sell it; sell it at once. I have always wanted to see you in one of

Worth's best gowns; you have such a lovely figure."

Upon this Serena burst into tears.

"What is the matter?"

"Oh, Helen, to tempt me to use what is not mine! How could you! And I have been so harassed."

Then Mrs. Clare saw that it was indeed serious, and, being a woman of sympathetic turn, and a dear lover of this friend, said: "Yes, I see; of course not. Quite impossible! How stupid of me! But, Rena, what do you yourself think?"

"I don't think; every one asks that. I want advice, advice."

"Well, suppose you were to get a detective and ask him to find your man, and then give him his ring."

"But what if he stole it! It may not be his ring."

Mrs. Clare felt inclined to use something like the exclamation employed by Cousin John. She refrained, and went on to state that perhaps to advertise the ring cautiously, asking for proof of ownership, might answer.

Now Serena saw a little light, and said eagerly: "Why, yes; how dull men are! The setting has the French hall-mark. No one could guess that. It would serve to find the real owner."

"Or the thief," said Mrs. Clare. "He would know."

"I forgot that; I really should not care. But I do not think he would come for it. He would consider it a trap. I must think about it."

Mrs. Clare had exhausted her wisdom, or did not care to suggest that the thief might send some one else to claim and identify the ring. They had another cup of tea, Miss Vernon assuring her friend that she was the only person who had given her practical advice. As to the rector she was reticent, being still a little sore. Cousin John had been simply absurd. "And, in fact," she said, "Helen, John is always a little—well—embarrassed. No; I should not say just that, dear, but unnatural. I think it grows on him."

Mrs. Clare looked up from a futile effort to balance a teaspoon on the lip of a tea-cup, and said: "Is n't that rather droll of a man of the world like Mr. Winterbourne? Do you know, Rena, I sometimes think — I mean, is it not even yet possible that —"

"No, Helen, it is not. Pardon my interruption; and, dear, you are rather fond of going back to this somewhat aged subject. Suppose we drop it. John and I made a friendly contract seven years ago. I am satisfied with my own life, and as for John, he is a confirmed bachelor."

"That is a curable malady, my dear Rena."

Here Miss Vernon let fall her handkerchief, and recovered it, but not very promptly, feeling, as she sat up, that her tendency to blush on slight occasion was a habit which seemed to be difficult to overcome. She said, with a smile: "Let us return to our diamond, Helen. I will think it over afresh. I wish I had asked John not to mention it. He evidently thought it an amusing tale. I do not."

"But apart, dear Rena, from your quite excessive scruples (oh, they are excessive), it is a thing

any one might be apt to relate.
I should."

" But you will not."

" No, of course not.   Ah, here
are the boys."

VII

MISS VERNON walked homeward in the twilight, feeling that in the multitude of counselors there is not always wisdom. Were they right, after all? Had she dealt with her conscience so as to make it useless in as small an affair as this? Or were these people all wrong? And what should she do?

Just what she had feared did happen. Cousin John wrote:

DEAR RENA: I have your note, but, unluckily, I could not resist telling the

story to a man at the club last night.
Upon my word, you are quite needlessly sensitive. Lock up the ring and
wait until I come back in November.
Time is a good counselor. In a week
or two, if you drop the matter, something will turn up.

Yours always,

J. W.

P.S. As soon as I heard from you I
wrote the man a note and asked him
not to tell the story; but who could
resist such a comic opportunity? Pardon me.

John assured her that something
would turn up. Something did turn
up; several things turned up. After days of distracting thought
Serena wrote in her diary:

[53]

At last I seem to see my way. I shall advertise. If in —— months no one appears to claim the ring I shall feel free to use it for charity.

It will be seen that Miss Vernon was unable to set down the number of months. Twenty-one years of undisputed ownership make good a land claim, as she knew. This did not require an immediate decision. She sent her maid with a carefully considered advertisement to the office of the " Day-Book," a journal which she took chiefly because the name pleased her, and because it had no illustrations and no Sunday issue. This was her advertisement:

Found, October 9, a diamond ring. Absolute proof of ownership required.

[54]

Letter to S. V., at this office, must accurately describe setting and fix value.

Here Serena hesitated, and finally added:

No reward will be asked.

With a mind now at ease, Miss Vernon invited Dr. Saffron and Mrs. Clare to dine two days later, and in the interval gave up her mind to the study of an English church controversy as to the use of incense, and whether the number of candles on the altar should be odd or even. This, with what she meant for a triumphant menu, occupied her for a time. The next day letters began to come. It was

[55]

like the answers to a newspaper charade. Before the day of the dinner she had three hundred and twenty-one letters. All made more or less elaborate guesses at plain gold, enamel, or pearl setting, and so on endlessly. All tried a shot at the value of the ring, and several came near enough. On the afternoon of her dinner she went to the city to get chocolate bonbons for dessert. Returning at dusk in the trolley, she heard two shop-girls talking.

"It must be the same. Just look here. Read that. The 'Herald' has two just lovely articles about it. You had n't seen it?

Why, where have you been?
Everybody 's talking about it, and
in the ' Day-Book ' there is an advertisement of the ring; it must
be the same ring. Seven of us
wrote letters to describe it — just
for fun."

"And suppose you had hit on
the right description?" said her
companion.

"Oh, that would be awful fun;
but law! one could n't take it."

"Oh, no. The thief, he might
describe it; but he 'd be afraid."

"Yes, but he might find out the
house and burgle it. If I was her
I 'd be dreadful scared. Think I 'd
move."

[57]

Serena Vernon grew cold with anticipative fear. "This is John's doing; how could he!"

"The advertisement does n't give her name," said girl number one. "I wish I was her. I 'd soon settle it, and I would n't be goose enough to cackle all over creation. Oh, the 'Herald' says her name is — oh, I forget. It 's a real romantic name, like it was out of a novel — oh, Serena Vernon. I 'll lend you the paper. Don't lose it. Here 's my station."

Miss Vernon sat up, a representative statue of all the outraged modesties of a retiring gentlewoman. "Oh, John," she murmured, "I hate you. What shall

[58]

I do?" She bought the "Herald," and read with increasing misery, in huge head-lines:

ROMANTICALLY AMAZING INCIDENT

WAS IT A TENDER ATTENTION TO THE LADY?
WAS HE REALLY A PICKPOCKET?
WHAT WILL SHE DO WITH IT?

A gentleman sits by a lady in a trolley. He is said to have stolen her porte-monnaie from her bag, and in doing so dropped in it a diamond ring valued at three thousand dollars. Loss of purse discovered on her return home. Ring found at bottom of her bag.

The heroine of this adventure is Miss Serena Vernon, a lady about forty-one

[59]

years of age, well known in society at
Denham. We hope to print her photograph to-morrow, with further particulars. Was he a thief? If so, the
advertisement in yesterday's "Day-
Book" may be an effort to induce the
man to call for his ring. A rather fee-
ble feminine device; or is there some
tender sentiment in the background?

Serena was half a mile past her
home when she ceased re-reading
this agreeable article and left the
car. What could she do? She
rang her bell, and, entering, found
a young man on a chair in the little
hall. He rose.

"Miss Vernon, I believe?"

"I am Miss Vernon. What is
it?"

"I represent the 'Daily Critic.' I want a few particulars in regard to the astounding incident of the diamond ring."

"Sir," said Miss Vernon, "this is an impertinence. What have you to do with my private affairs?"

"Then it was true? Thank you, ma'am. Any further facts would gratify the public."

For a moment the well-bred gentlewoman was struck dumb with astonishment. "Will you be so good as to leave my house?" and she approached the hall door.

"Yes, ma'am. Then you don't board. You live alone."

"Leave my house."

"But, ma'am, is it true that the

gentleman is known to you? Or is it true that he has returned the purse and only kept a —"

"Will you go!" cried Miss Vernon.

"But, ma'am — excuse me, ma'am, the public is interested. Why not give us the real story and let us contradict that nonsense in the 'Herald.'"

"Will you go!" said Miss Vernon, "or, or —" She was at her wits' end. "Shall I, must I call the dog? Towser! Towser!" she cried.

She had a fine fear of dogs, big or little, and, needless to say, possessed none.

"Certainly, ma'am; sorry to have intruded."

" Well, go, then."

Never before in her life had she been so abrupt to man or woman. He went out, and paused under the next electric light to make a note of her apparent age and costume.

VIII

SERENA entered her little library, and, throwing herself into a chair, sat twisting her gloves, angry and miserable. "Oh for a man!" she exclaimed.

Here she was still sitting when Mrs. Clare and Dr. Saffron appeared. Serena, hastily regaining her composure, rose as her friends entered, and excused herself for having been late in returning from the city. The doctor, in turn, apologized. He had not replied to her

note of invitation until two hours
ago, as a consultation had called
him away, and he had been absent
three days. Her invitations to
dine answered themselves. When
were they ever refused? There
was a certain harmony in the dress,
face, and figure of this complacent
little gentleman, whose self-as-
surance carried everywhere a com-
forting sense of belief in his
competence to deal with all human
ills. An underestimate of the diffi-
culty of the most difficult of professions, and an overestimate of
Roderick Saffron, had served, with
rather too sympathetic manners, to
win for him a large practice and
to make of him a general favor-

[65]

ite. Children liked him; mothers
adored him; and if men liked or
trusted him less completely it was
of small moment in general practice, where it is the verdict of
women which decides the fortunes
of a doctor.

Mrs. Clare glanced at her friend's
half-mended disorder of face, and
said: "Don't hurry, dear. I will
go up-stairs with you. The doctor
will excuse me."

"Certainly," he replied.

They had been gone a minute
when the maid appeared and told
the doctor that two persons, men,
were in the entry, insisting on seeing Miss Vernon. Would he speak
to them? She had said her mis-

tress was engaged. They said they would wait. They would not go away. The doctor went out, and in a few minutes came back apparently amused. When the ladies returned, he said:

" My dear Miss Serena, we have had two reporters here. I saw them. They had some supremely ridiculous tale about a diamond; one man wanted your photograph. I simply told them the tale they had heard was not true; it was most absurd. And you may imagine what I said as to a photograph. I have not the honor to possess one myself. They said the story should be contradicted to-morrow, and went away."

"They went away!" said Miss Vernon. "And you told them it was not true—not true!"

"Yes; they were a trifle obstinate, but these fellows are so used to being received with, may I say, rudeness and disgust, that a little civility always disarms them. You may be quite at your ease. They will contradict the story."

"But I am not at all at my ease, and it is true," said Serena. Whereupon she related the facts to her astonished physician. "What will they think of me?"

"Well," he said, "I have innocently fibbed for you, and a very good thing, too. But pardon me if I ask what you mean to do

[68]

about the ring. Had I been at home you no doubt would have done me the honor to ask my advice."

Mrs. Clare smiled unworded comment. "Give it now," she said.

The doctor was by habit inclined to learn what form of advice would be agreeable before venturing to restate it in his own words. He hesitated, and then said: "To know what you have thought or done in this strange affair would reinforce my decision with knowledge."

"It is too late," said Mrs. Clare. "Our friend has advertised for the owner of the diamond."

"I could have predicted Miss Vernon's course from my long acquaintance with her character."

Mrs. Clare was delighted. She, too, had been silently predictive, but not as to her friend.

"The thief will not come," added the doctor.

"Oh, I hope he will," said Serena. "No, I hope he will not. I want the real owner to claim it. I have had a bushel of letters. Suppose no one comes? What am I to do?"

"There is our village hospital," ventured the doctor.

"You are as bad as my rector," said Serena, smiling.

"Let us wait a little," said Mrs. Clare. She still had hopes of seeing her friend in one of Worth's gowns. "At the worst, Rena," she

[70]

added, "you can give it to me. I will put it away for Harry's wife, and as he is now only six years old, the question would be ethically settled by the time he is, say, twenty-eight."

"How ingeniously proper, how judicial!" said the doctor.

"Thanks, Helen," said Serena; "there is something in that. I think Solomon must have owed his wisdom to the numberless ladies of his household."

"Yes, if wisdom be the child of experience," laughed Mrs. Clare.

The doctor made a mental record of Miss Vernon's compliment to the wits of woman for future use, when it might be desirable to explain his suave compliance with the views of some too resolute mother.

"Read no papers for a week," said Helen Clare. "That is my advice."

"The 'Churchman' or the 'Guardian' might be safe," said the doctor.

Serena smiled, and they went out to dinner.

IX

THE dinner was an unusual success, and Miss Vernon awakened next morning enough at ease to read a dozen more letters with some sense of amusement.

The next day two women reporters called, and an evening paper printed as a portrait of Miss Vernon a full-length of a variety actress, twice divorced.

A little later, the cook was offered a dollar for particulars of Miss Vernon's life. Serena began to think of moving.

In the afternoon the rector called, and how soothing, how satisfactory it was that the "Globe" had contradicted the extravagant statements of the "Herald"!

Miss Vernon was unable to feel quite satisfied, for, after all, the story was true. When asked by the Rev. Angelo King how it came to be denied by one of her own household, she explained the doctor's share in the matter, the rector interjecting at intervals, "Really! Really!" At last he said: "How painful to have been put in the position of appearing to sustain a deviation from truth!"

Miss Vernon felt that she was overstating her disapproval. She held in the background behind her conscience a feeling that now the thing would cease to excite public comment. She said as much.

"The doctor has clearly bungled," said the rector — "in fact, has assumed to know what he did not. But, my dear Miss Serena, if Dr. Saffron had a too childlike confidence in himself, *we* know that out of the mouths of babes cometh wisdom." He was so well pleased with this that he repeated it for the benefit of Mrs. Clare, who came in as he spoke.

Serena saw his satisfaction at this use of biblical quotation. She did not like it, but was tardily amused, knowing that her rector

greatly disliked the doctor. Mrs.
Clare knew why, but had always
laughingly declined to explain to
Serena. After this they discussed
the Montana mission, when the rector at last rose. He said: "Has
a way opened to you—I mean about
the diamond?"

She said, "No," but then apologized so gently for what she called
her abrupt treatment of his advice
that he went away seeing the reredos a little more distinctly.

Then for a time the papers ceased
from troubling, the letters came
no more, and there was a lull in
the affair of the diamond ring.
Serena put it in her strong box in

[76]

the bank, and had additional bolts placed on her first-floor windows. The burglar still haunted her uncomfortably. Soon after, a letter came from a friend in Santa Barbara, which much annoyed her. She showed it and the clipping it inclosed to Mrs. Clare. On this Mrs. Clare asked her if she knew the game called Russian scandal. Serena had played it when young.

"Well, my dear, the newspapers play it all the time. It would seem easy to copy a paragraph accurately; but here you see what happens. This fine tale has gone over all the land, and this is the result." She read aloud:

[77]

" ' A very beautiful Quaker lady in Durham, Pennsylvania, was followed into a car by a gentleman. He let fall into her bag a diamond ring valued at four thousand dollars. A romantic termination is probably to follow this unusual form of wooing. It is said he took her purse when he dropped his ring into her bag. Perhaps he wanted a *gage d'amour.*'— *Santa Barbara Journal.*

" Another account says the brooch — or was it a ring ?— will reappear in the form of a reredos in the church at Durham, and that she has refused the gentleman and also refused to return his ring.

" Serena, that rector has been gabbling; observe the reredos."

" Well," said Serena, " it does

seem only too likely. Burn it, dear.
Men are all alike."

"They are all alike, are they?
Even John?"

"Yes, all. This is my new tea,
Helen. Try it."

On Saturday, a week later, Miss
Vernon received a letter from
Tampa, Florida.

DEAR RENA: The ducks were not
at Currituck, and why I came hither I
do not know, except that one must go
somewhere. I have been eating hum-
ble-pie because of my folly, and, my
dear cousin, it never agrees with me.
I have read those blank papers, and
the denial, and the advertisement.
What a coil! I am sorry if, as is
stated, you authorized the contradiction.

6

It was not like you. And who is the re-
ported Mr. Butterworth who was inter-
viewed and represented you? I did
not suspect you of this form of dupli-
city! Never ask a newspaper to say it
has lied, or, except in politics, to say
another paper has lied. My poor Rena,
if I were to cowhide this fellow he would
only contrive worse things, and would
swear, what is true, that the main fact
is correct; and, really, to lick a reporter
for coarse-minded misuse of facts would
be valueless, or involve a too chronic
use of this ultimate resort. After all,
I am the one to blame. I am coming
back at once. Do not move further in
the matter.

Your affectionate cousin,

JOHN.

"Well," said Serena, aloud, "if

anything were needed to make it all seem worse, this would. First John talks, then my doctor talks, then my rector talks; and they think *we* gossip."

That night Serena wrote in her diary:

Yes, I do believe I have been wicked enough to want to have some one suffer for this outrage — some one besides poor, innocent me, who have lived in what Helen calls a cocoon of privacy. Alas! I think I might once have married, but the unpleasant publicity of it all seemed so shocking, and now I am *affichéed* like an opera-dancer. It does seem too atrocious. I shall never forgive you, John, never.

Miss Serena in all her gentle life

[81]

had never so hated man or woman as to need to forgive. John was safe enough. The following Monday she wrote in her diary:

The local express brought a pile of late English journals. How thoughtful of John! Also by mail came an article blue-penciled — why   blue? — from "Views and Reviews, a Journal in the Interest of the Past and the Future of the Ulterior Womanhood." That seems elaborate. The article is on my diamond — I mean on what John calls the "Great Diamond Trust."

"This curious story has its moral aspects. If the lady had not been so silly as to be needlessly civil to a man she would not have been in her present conscientious quandary."

How does any one know that I have

[82]

a conscience, or was civil, or am in a quandary?

The next heading is, "The Anti-Marriage League," and, by way of contrast, an advertisement of the "Company to Insure Permanence in the Marriage State."

Good gracious! it is needed. I suppose there would be an examination on looks, temper, and money. I thought to show it to John. I do not think I shall. It sounds too like John. I do not mean that he is not refined. Mem.: The use of a diary is a temptation to be foolish.

Tuesday. Delicious bunch of snipe from John, and a telegram. He is on his way North. What nonsense to *wire!* How easily one's language becomes debased! Mem.: To avoid this word.

[83]

X

ON Wednesday morning that
which ever since the advertisement was unlooked for, but
probable, did occur. As Serena
turned into the lane which led to
her house, a slight, quiet, well-
dressed man crossed the street,
took off his hat, and said: "I have
the honor to address Miss Vernon?"

"That is my name, but if you
are a reporter —"

"I am not, madam, a reporter.
I am Charles Lytton of Sedgely,

Alabama. I am the owner of the diamond which I see has been, must have been, the source of anxiety and annoyance. The newspapers have, I grieve to say — "

Miss Vernon was on her guard. The man's tones lacked that indefinable something in the way of inflection which should have gone with what seemed to be carefully chosen language — a little too careful; nor had he the accent of the South. She interrupted him.

"Come in," she said, quite resolute, but also somewhat nervous.

He followed her into the library and cast a glance of swift survey about the room. They sat down, Serena near the bell.

[85]

"I lost, I should say my wife lost, this ring, her mother's marriage gift. It was stolen on a French steamer, the *Gascoigne*, last year. Of course it is very dear to me. You will pardon my emotion."

Serena pardoned the emotion, but reflected on the size of the departed Mrs. Lytton's finger.

"Here is the description of the ring," he continued; "I have written it out."

Serena read and re-read it. It was accurate. She was clear at once that either this was the true owner, or, as was probable, that he represented the thief. But how to be sure?

[86]

"'And now, madam, . . . have the kindness
to give me my ring.'"

"And now, madam," he said, not waiting for her decision, "have the kindness to give me my ring."

She made no reply except to look up and then once more to consider the memoranda. These were written on a rather soiled half-sheet of ruled note-paper. This caused Serena to have a prejudicial distrust of which she was conscious and a little ashamed. Time was now what she most wanted. She said: "It appears to be — I have no doubt it is all correct.[1] The ring is in the bank."

"I have to leave town to-day," he said. "If you will go with me

[1] Diary: "This was not quite true. I am sorry I said it."

[89]

to the bank you will add to my obligations."

Miss Vernon replied with calmness: "I fear that in so large a matter I must ask for further information, and, pardon me, for some personal identification."

Then he saw that he had lost the game. He rose. "I should think that needless. However, I will wait over two days" ("Why two?" thought Serena), "and on Friday will return with my friend Mr. Seeley, the cashier of the Mechanics' Trust. Will that answer? And may we set twelve o'clock? Do you know Mr. Seeley?"

"I do not," she returned. "I shall be here at that hour."

"I must leave at one forty·five.

Will you kindly have the ring
ready?"

If he did not come the ring would
be safe. If he did, Mr. Seeley, a
well-known citizen, would be present, the man vouched for, and she
relieved. At all events, John
should be there. All this passed
through her mind before she repeated, "Yes, the ring shall be
here, and I shall be most pleased
to get rid of it. Good morning";
and he went away.

A little later came Mrs. Clare, to
whom Miss Vernon related the interview, adding: "And now,
Helen, how does it strike you?"

"Was he possibly a reporter, a
gossip burglar?"

"Goodness! Helen, no. I should

prefer a real burglar. Tell me, dear, you do not think he was that; that would —"

"No, I do not. But he will not come. Do you know Mr. Seeley, dear? I do."

"No; but in any case John will be here."

"Why is not John always here, or you there?"

"I wish you would not, Helen."

"Would not what?"

"You know well enough."

"You will marry him, Rena."

"No, never."

"Then he will marry you."

"It is too late. I am —"

"My dear, have the kindness to consult that oracle, the looking-

[92]

glass. You dear, sweet, shy, silly creature! How pretty you are when you blush!"

"Don't, please."

"Well, as you like. I must go."

At dusk came a note from Mrs. Clare.

I have seen Frank Seeley. He does not know your man.

"I thought as much," said Serena. "Why did I not think of this? How clever she is!"

XI

WHEN John Winterbourne arrived next day, he said: "Come for a drive, Serena. Don't talk now. Get a warm wrap. My dog-cart is on the avenue."

When they were far out in the country, he said: "Here is an apology from that editorial scamp to whom my friend told the story. He regrets, etc.; will make it all right in to-morrow's paper. I said no, he must hold his tongue; that was all I asked."

"Thank you, John. That was right. I must have no more of it."

"Of course, Rena, the editor was out of town. He always is when these things happen."

"Are there no decent journals, John?"

"Certainly. The 'Day-Book' and the 'Episcopal Recorder.' Oh, others, too, Rena. Don't look so grave. What a glorious day! But what of the diamond?"

Then she told him of her latest interview. It was now his turn to look grave.

"Rena, the man came from your thief. He did not expect to succeed. He will not return on Friday, at least not at the time set.

He wanted to be sure that you would have the ring in your house. I say, Rena, you have a spare room?"

"Yes."

"Will you take me in for a day or two?"

Rena hesitated for an instant, and said: "Yes, John, of course. But what is it? What do you fear?"

"I do not know. I will speak to the police."

"No; oh, no!"

"Why not?"

"He will think I set a trap for him."

"And why not?"

"But, John, it will be in the papers again, and I shall have to

[96]

go to court, and more reporters will come, and, after all, I shall still have the ring, and there we are just where we began."

"Rena, you want a man to take care of you. You wear too tight shoes on your conscience. You are a moral tenderfoot."

"A what, John?"

"Too much conscience, Rena."

"You are right, I dare say — I mean about my conscience."

"Possibly it has had so little sin to attend to that it has become too — well, too concentrated."

"What nonsense, John!"

"Cousin Rena, are you past seeing the fun of the Diamond Trust?"

"Pretty nearly."

"Best get all the amusement out of it you can."

"There is n't anything new, John, is there?" She was alarmed.

"No, only pure fun. I cut out a few paragraphs from Southern papers. Like to look at them, Rena?"

"No, I should not."

"But, Rena, there is one — just take the reins; they 'll go along."

"I shall do no such thing."

"Well, here it is. I forgot — stuck it in my waistcoat pocket."

Miss Vernon took it reluctantly, saying: "I shall read this and no more. Helen Clare says it is a dreadful thing to come into the changeless peace of life like mine.

[98]

It was so prettily worded, but when she went on to say such an event was disheveling, that did seem to me an odd use of English."

"Rather," said John, touching up the leader. "Read it aloud. How could it have got so mixed up?"

Serena read:

"A well-known society woman in Rahway was in the habit of going to New York daily on a trolley. She observed a gentleman who was always on the same car with her. He watched her so constantly as to embarrass her, contriving always, soon or late, to sit beside her. On several occasions she found at the end of her journey that jewels had been placed in the reticule she carried.

One was a diamond worth a thousand dollars; once it was a pearl ring; once an opal ring. She is sure these were put in her bag by the gentleman above mentioned. When she ceased to travel on this line, every second day some jewel was left at the house by mail or by express. Miss Varnum ["Gracious!" exclaimed Serena, "Varnum!"] is the lady's name. Strangely enough, under this opulent persecution ["'Opulent' is a fine adjective, Rena," interposed John] Miss Varnum's nerves have given way, and she is now about to consult the distinguished neurologist, Dr. von Neuron.

"That is certainly worthy of the newspaper novelist," said Serena. "It would be curious to see how from the 'Herald's' horrid account it got by degrees to this."

"It gives one a certain disrespect for history, Rena. I won't ask you to read the others. They would curdle your young blood. Well, I will come on Friday, and, by the by, I had a day at Currituck. You will get your ducks this evening. Don't overcook them."

"As if I could allow such a thing, John!"

"I told Tom to leave with them a case of Corton Vieux. I have just got my importation. Don't drink it for two months."

"John, that kind of thing must stop. You know —"

"It never will stop."

[101]

"You nearly ran into that wagon."

"I did; it was your nonsense, Rena. You did not stir. You are the least nervous woman I ever drove."

"Do you drive many — many women?"

"Several," said John.

Serena was silent, and then said:

"How the leaves are falling!"

"Too fast," said John.

Serena meditated.

XII

JOHN'S bag came that evening, and the wine and the ducks. He followed them at noon, in time for luncheon, on Friday. No visitors appeared. In the afternoon he lighted a cigar and went out at the back of the house to think a little. Serena had begged him to smoke in her library. This was unusual. She rather liked the odor of tobacco, but entertained antique prejudices in regard to the habit, as her doctor knew to his postpran-

[103]

dial discomfort. John had two sub-
jects for reflection. One he put
aside. The other was answered in
a measure by the revolver in his
breast pocket. He walked on,
keenly scrutinizing those who went
by. About dusk he observed a
large man under a slouched felt hat
and in a loose cloak, a rather un-
common garment. He was smok-
ing. He paused a moment opposite to Serena's lane, and then
continued on his way. About half
a block farther he crossed over,
and, as John had lingered, they
approached each other. John
dropped his cigar behind him, and,
holding a fresh one in his hand,
paused, asking in his most civil

way for a light. The other gave
him his cigar without words. As
John lighted his own, he let fall
the stranger's cigar. On this he
apologized profusely, and offered
his open cigar-case. The man
helped himself, and said, "Much
obliged." As he secured a light
from John's cigar, it was too dark
to see well, but the illumination of
the two bright tips lighted up a
coarse face in flashes. The man
had a large wart on his left cheek.
John said, "You will find the cigar
good," and moved on murmuring
to himself: "We are to have two,
then. Oh, Rena, your fear of
wholesome publicity may prove to
be a pretty business. A few police-

men would — well, I think I can
arrange it. And where is Mr.
Lytton? This beats tarpon-fishing." He made a long circuit and
reëntered the house at the back
door, throwing away his cigar.

At six-thirty the door-bell rang,
and the servant announced Mr.
Lytton. Serena rose, and said under her breath, "Tell Mr. John
after the man comes in."

She was amazed to feel so tran-
quil. Was it John? Meanwhile
Mr. Lytton in the hall reopened
the street door so as to leave it
slightly ajar, and a moment later
was seated at the fire, while Serena
listened for her cousin's step on the
stair. He had gone quietly down

[106]

the back stairway, warned the wo-. men to keep the back door locked, and waited a moment.

Mr. Lytton said: "Mr. Seeley is out of town. I have come for the ring. I cannot consent, ma'am, to your delaying its return." His tone was peremptory.

Serena glanced at the half-closed door which led into the dining-room, and hearing no sign of John, became anxious, but, to her surprise, not at all alarmed. She had failed John once. He had never failed her. Mr. Lytton arose, looked into the back room, and returned without explaining his cautious inspection. At this moment the front door was heard to close

[107]

gently. The thief of the trolley-car entered. Serena rose. The newcomer caught her by the wrist, and said: "Now, no nonsense, miss; I want my ring."

Serena was never timid in an emergency. She said: "Be so good as not to clasp my wrist so hard. I can't get away."

"Give me my ring!"

"It is not yours," she said boldly, "and I have not got it with me." She was very quiet, almost cool. John had it.

"Where is it?"

"That you will not know until you prove that you own it."

"You had best tell us, or —"

"I will die first."

[108]

"Both men were too old at the game to hesitate."

At this moment the door was thrown open, and John cried out, "Hands up," the gleaming steel barrel of a revolver emphasizing the order. Both men were too old at the game to hesitate. They obeyed him, and Serena fell into a chair, not too scared to fail of admiration of the handsome figure in a velvet lounging-jacket. Said John, "A single shot will call the police, but I never miss."

Serena was amused, even at this critical moment, at the absurdity of the two scamps with their hands in the air.

"Move a little nearer, you fellows," said John. "So, that will do; now we will talk. Be so

[111]

good as to remember that a shot
will cripple one of you and call the
officers. Now answer me. Where
did you get that ring? You, the
big chap."

"It is mine."

"Stuff! Don't trifle. Answer.
If you tell the truth and I can
prove it, you may go. By the
way, you other fellow, I do not
want you. You may go; but
hands up and shut the door after
you."

The gentleman in question made
no reply except to obey. He
closed the library door behind him,
and was wise enough to carry off
Serena's seal jacket and John's
overcoat. The front door shut
clamorously.

"And now," said John, "I want to know. Don't stir. Keep up your hands — higher. It is a trifle fatiguing. Moses found it so."

"Oh, John!"

"Be quiet, Rena. This gentleman has the floor. Come, now, out with it. The truth or the penitentiary."

"You can't prove nothing."

"What about that pocket-book?"

"And my luck-penny?"

"Do, Rena, keep quiet."

"Will you let me go if I own up square?"

"I will."

"How shall I be sure?"

"Damn it, you fool! You can't help telling, and I have promised. You have got to trust the inconceivable probability of having to do with a gentleman."

"Well, I stole it in New York. It was part of the plunder in the big Schmitt burglary last May."

"Who has the proof?"

"The police in New York has the description. Now let me go."

"Not much. Here, Rena, write. I will dictate:

"POLICE HEADQUARTERS, NEW YORK:
"Found, set in a gold ring with French hall-mark of 1838, a diamond, value about eight hundred dollars, two and a half carats. Schmitt burglary. Instant answer. Repeat message."

Serena wrote as he dictated.
"Read it aloud. . . . That will do.

[114]

Now put on your wraps and take that telegram yourself to the nearest station. Take your maid. Give the operator five dollars, and promise five more for an immediate answer. Wait for it. Go out the back way. I will amuse our guest. Tell the police outside to wait. If the reply is as it should be, send them away. They will understand."

She read over the telegram, repeated her cousin's directions, and left at once.

XIII

"AND now," said John, "a moment." He came closer, put the pistol to the man's head, and with his left hand extracted a revolver from the breast pocket of the thief's coat. He let it fall into his own pocket, and said: "Sit down; drop your hands; you must be tired. Let us talk. What is your name? Any alias will do. I want a convenient handle."

"Don't know what for. Hall, Joe Hall, will do." He was angry and sullen.

"What 's your special line of business? I take it Miss Vernon's purse was a little side sport. The moral is, Keep to your own line; don't speculate. By the way, have you kept that purse?"

"Yes; I use it myself. I 'll chuck it into the bargain. Money 's gone, of course. There 's a queer penny; it 's in it now. Oh, come to think, my gal tried a receipt there was. Pretty nigh pizened me. Ain't been the same man since. You can have the purse."

"Put the purse on that chair." He did so. "Variety of knowledge is of value in all the professions, Mr. Hall."

"What?"

"Well, that luck-penny is worth about one hundred dollars; a rare coin."

"Gosh! I missed it, did n't I?"

"Yes, you did. Suppose we talk. We have two or three hours. If you are not lying you are safe."

"I was on the square, by —"

"We can't sit here for an hour or two in silence. Don't swear, not here at least. Tell me your biggest burgle."

What followed was sufficiently entertaining, and would have set up in detective and anti-detective crime literature a dozen small story-tellers. Joe, beginning to feel safe, was flattered and at last fluent. John was delighted — appreciative of the joy of risks.

"If you were to put all this cleverness into some regular, honest work — why not, Mr. Hall?"

"Would n't be any fun in it."

"No, I see. Pray go on."

"Well, shall I tell you how I stole the — well, no good to name them — the pearls last year, and what came of it?" He laughed, now quite at ease.

"A good story," said John.

"There is a better one."

"What 's that?"

"Oh, about the watermelon bank. Tom Crocker, he used to keep all his money in a watermelon. And Tom's grandmother, she give away that watermelon to —"

At this moment Serena, red and handsome, returned breathless.

"It's all right," she cried; "he told the truth. Here is the telegram; read it."

"DETECTIVE OFFICE, POLICE HEAD-
QUARTERS, NEW YORK.

"Hold thief if you have him.

"Not I," said John.

"Oh, no," said Serena.

"Description correct. Any clue to the ruby bracelet?"

Joe grinned. "I did n't drop that in the bag, sir."

"No. Police gone, Serena?"

"There are none."

"Never were," said John.

"Euchred all round," said Joe.

"Now, my man," said John, "you may go. Your story will never be

[120]

finished. This is very like compounding a felony — but Miss Vernon is averse to publicity."

"Me, too," said Joe, much relieved. "Never told a lie in my life."

"Until now," said John. "Get out of this."

"Good night, sir"; and Joe, accompanied to the door by John, departed in great haste.

XIV

JOHN came back. It was ten
o'clock. "Rena," he said, "you
may now comfortably rock to sleep
that uneasy, over-educated conscience. You want a care-taker,
Rena; you must have been born an
orphan. How I am to settle with
the New York police is past my
comprehension."

"John, I am, as always, in your
debt."

"Then pay," he said.

"I cannot; I never can."

"Try; an effort at honesty is always possible, even for the most depraved."

"What can I do, John?"

"You know well enough."

"Yes," she said, looking him full in the eyes, a little flushed, a look of tender sadness in the face lines. "I — I cannot pretend to misunderstand you. I — I have liked you ever since we were children. I know how great, how undeserved, is all your love and patience, but—"

"But what, Rena?"

"Oh, I — I am not sure, and — not to be sure would be unjust, wicked. It is such a — I cannot."

"Say *will* not, Rena."

[123]

"But I do not want to say that. It seems hard. It is always you who are good and helpful, and it is I who have no way to thank you."

"But there is a way."

"Yes, I know, I know. I — I can't, John."

Then John Winterbourne bent over her and took her hand and caressed it with a light touch of his own, and said : "Well, my dear Rena, never mind me. Unless it is to make you also happy, as I should be, I do not want you to say 'Yes.' Either you care for — no, love me, or you do not; and if not, let us go on as we have done. It is only

[124]

one more disappointment. Were
the ducks good, Rena?"

"Oh, John, when — how can
you! When I am hurt, troubled,
because I cannot — to talk — about
— about ducks."

"Then damn the ducks!"

"John!"

"Suppose you go to bed, Rena;
you are nervous."

"I never was nervous in my
life."

"Your eyes are red."

"They are not."

"Go to bed, dear. May I smoke
here? Where is your last 'Spec-
tator'?"

There was in this cold ending of

an imminent love-scene something
which Rena felt to be harsh and
unfit. She cared most truly for
this man, and knew, too, he was
acting in order to set her at ease.
She moved toward the door. Then
she turned and said:

"I do not like, John, to be always weighed down with debt.
Things cannot go on as they have
done."

"My dear Rena, you can send
the scale flying and make me the
abject, hopeless debtor. One
word, dear — no, three."

"I cannot. Indeed I cannot.
"Good night, John." She left the
room. He heard her footfall on
the stairs, heard the sound of win-

dows closed and of bolts shot. The servants had gone to bed; the house was still.

John Winterbourne lighted a cigar and sat down. He read no journal; a half-hour went by. He sat up of a sudden. Was that Rena? He went out into the dark hall-way. Then he heard Rena's voice out of the gloom overhead:

"John!"

"What is it, Rena? Anything wrong?"

"No."

"What the deuce is it?"

"Nothing. You don't think those burglars could —"

"Dear child! It is not eleven Go to bed."

[127]

"Good night, Cousin John. I — I want to say something — I cannot — "

"Very good, dear. I will come up."

"No, please not. You must not, John."

"Oh, all right. What is it? Won't it keep?"

"Please to go away before I come down to-morrow."

"By George! Really! Certainly, Rena. 6 A.M.?"

"John!" This was very low.

"Well?"

"I think I love you."

"Oh, Rena!"

"And come back to dinner, John."

[128]

"God bless you, Rena," he said as he heard the quick retreat of feet overhead.

Then John Winterbourne went back to the library, where he sat down and wrote a letter to Serena Vernon; but what he wrote I do not know.